THE DIAMOND MAKER

BY

ARTHUR B. REEVE

British Library Cataloguing-in-Publication Data
A catalogue record for this book is available from the
British Library

Arthur Benjamin Reeve

Arthur Benjamin Reeve was born on 15th October 1880 in New York, USA.

Reeve received his University education at Princeton and upon graduating enrolled at the New York Law School. However, his career was not destined to be in the field of Law. Between 1910 and 1918 he produced 82 short stories for Cosmopolitan magazine featuring his super-sleuth Professor Craig Kennedy. Kennedy is sometimes referred to as "The American Sherlock Holmes" due to his astounding ability at crime solving and his Watson-like sidekick Walter Jameson, a newspaper reporter. These characters featured in 18 novels, some of which were pseudo-novels stitched together from various short stories.

During this period he also began authoring screenplays, beginning with *The Exploits of Elaine* (1914). By the end of this decade his film career was at its peak with his name appearing on seven films, most of them serials and three of them starring Harry Houdini. Due to the film industry's migration to the west coast of America and Reeve's desire to remain in the east he produced less and less work for film. However, in 1927 he entered into a contract to write film scenarios for notorious millionaire-murderer, Harry K. Thaw, on the subject of fake spiritualists. The deal resulted in a lawsuit when Thaw refused to pay. In late 1928, Reeve declared bankruptcy.

Reeve continued to write detective stories for pulp magazines, but also covered many celebrated crime cases for various newspapers, including the murder of William Desmond Taylor, and the trial of Lindbergh baby kidnapper, Bruno Hauptmann. During the 1930s he became an anti-rackets crusader and produced a work of history on the subject titled *The Golden Age of Crime* (1931).

In 1932 he moved to Trenton to be near his alma mater. He died on 9th August 1936.

THE DIAMOND MAKER

"I've called, Professor Kennedy, to see if we can retain you in a case which I am sure will tax even your resources. Heaven knows it has taxed ours."

The visitor was a large, well-built man. He placed his hat on the table and, without taking off his gloves, sat down in an easy chair which he completely filled.

"Andrews is my name--third vice-president of the Great Eastern Life Insurance Company. I am the nominal head of the company's private detective force, and though I have some pretty clever fellows on my staff we've got a case that, so far, none of us has been able to unravel. I'd like to consult you about it."

Kennedy expressed his entire willingness to be consulted, and after the usual formalities were over, Mr. Andrews proceeded.

"I suppose you are aware that the large insurance companies maintain quite elaborate detective forces and follow very keenly such of the cases of their policy-holders as look at all suspicious. This case which I wish to put in your hands is that of Mr. Solomon Morowitch, a wealthy Maiden Lane jeweller. I suppose you have read something in the papers about his sudden death and the strange robbery of his safe?"

"Very little," replied Craig. "There hasn't been much to read."

"Of course not, of course not," said Mr. Andrews with some show of gratification. "I flatter myself that we have pulled the wires so as to keep the thing out of the papers as much as possible. We don't want to frighten the quarry till the net is spread. The point is, though, to find out who is the quarry. It's most baffling."

"I am at your service," interposed Craig quietly, "but you will have to enlighten me as to the facts in the case. As to that, I know no more than the newspapers."

"Oh, certainly, certainly. That is to say, you know nothing at all and can approach it without bias." He paused and then, seeming to notice something in Craig's manner, added hastily: "I'll be perfectly frank with you. The policy in question is for one hundred thousand dollars, and is incontestable. His wife is the beneficiary. The company is perfectly willing to pay, but we want to be sure that it is all straight first. There are certain suspicious circumstances that in justice to ourselves we think should be cleared up. That is all--believe me. We are not seeking to avoid an honest liability."

"What are these suspicious circumstances?" asked Craig, apparently satisfied with the explanation.

"This is in strict confidence, gentlemen," began Mr. Andrews. "Mr. Morowitch, according to the story as it comes to us, returned home late one night last week, apparently from his office, in a very weakened, a semiconscious, condition. His family physician, Doctor Thornton, was summoned, not at once, but shortly. He pronounced Mr. Morowitch to be suffering from a congestion of the lungs that was very like a sudden attack of pneumonia.

"Mr. Morowitch had at once gone to bed, or at least was in bed, when the doctor arrived, but his condition grew worse so rapidly that the doctor hastily resorted to oxygen, under which treatment he seemed to revive. The doctor had just stepped out to see another patient when a hurry call was sent to him that Mr. Morowitch was rapidly sinking. He died before the doctor could return. No statement whatever concerning the cause of his sudden illness was made by Mr. Morowitch, and the death-certificate, a copy of which I have, gives pneumonia as the cause of death. One of our men has seen Doctor Thornton, but has been able to get nothing out of him. Mrs. Morowitch was the only person with her, husband at the time."

There was something in his tone that made me take particular note of this last fact, especially as he paused for an instant.

"Now, perhaps there would be nothing surprising about it all, so far at least, were it not for the fact that the following morning, when his junior partner, Mr. Kahan, opened the place of business, or rather went to it, for it was to remain closed, of course, he found that during the night someone had visited it. The lock on the great safe, which contained thousands of dollars' worth of diamonds, was intact; but in the top of the safe a huge hole was found--an irregular, round hole, big enough to put your foot through. Imagine it, Professor Kennedy, a great hole in a safe that is made of chrome steel, a safe that, short of a safety-deposit vault, ought to be about the strongest thing on earth.

"Why, that steel would dull and splinter even the finest diamond-drill before it made an impression. The mere taking out and refitting of drills into the brace would be a most lengthy process. Eighteen or twenty hours is the time by actual test which it would take to bore such a hole through those laminated plates, even if there were means of exerting artificial pressure. As for the police, they haven't even a theory yet."

"And the diamonds"

"All gone--everything of any value was gone. Even the letter-files were ransacked. His desk was broken open, and papers of some nature had been taken out of it. Thorough is no name for the job. Isn't that enough to arouse suspicion?"

"I should like to see that safe," was all Kennedy said.

"So you shall, so you shall," said Mr. Andrews. "Then we may retain you in our service? My car is waiting downstairs. We can go right down to Maiden Lane if you wish."

"You may retain me on one condition," said Craig without moving. "I am to be free to get at the truth whether it benefits or hurts the company, and the case is to be entirely in my hands."

"Hats on," agreed Mr. Andrews, reaching in his vest pocket and pulling out three or four brevas. "My chauffeur is quite a driver. He can almost beat the subway down."

"First, to my laboratory," interposed Craig. "It will take only a few minutes."

We drove up to the university and stopped on the campus while Craig hurried into the Chemistry Building to get something.

"I like your professor of criminal science;" said Andrews to me, blowing a huge fragrant cloud of smoke.

I, for my part, liked the vice-president. He was a man who seemed thoroughly to enjoy life, to have most of the good things, and a capacity for getting out of them all that was humanly possible. He seemed to be particularly enjoying this Morowitch case.

"He has solved some knotty cases," was all I said. "I've come to believe there is no limit to his resourcefulness."

"I hope not. He's up against a tough one this trip, though, my boy."

I did not even resent the "my boy." Andrews was one of those men in whom we newspaper writers instinctively believe. I knew that it would be "pens lifted" only so long

7

as the case was incomplete. When the time comes with such men they are ready to furnish us the best "copy" in the world.

Kennedy quickly rejoined us, carrying a couple of little glass bottles with ground-glass stoppers.

Morowitch & Co. was, of course, closed when we arrived, but we had no trouble in being admitted by the Central Office man who had been detailed to lock the barn door after the horse was stolen. It was precisely as Mr. Andrews had said. Mr. Kahan showed us the safe. Through the top a great hole had been made--I say made, for at the moment I was at a loss to know whether it had been cut, drilled, burned, blown out, or what-not.

Kennedy examined the edges of the hole carefully, and just the trace of a smile of satisfaction flitted over his face as he did so. Without saying a word he took the glass stopper out of the larger bottle which he had brought and poured the contents on the top of the safe near the hole. There it lay, a little mound of reddish powder.

Kennedy took a little powder of another kind from the other bottle and lighted it with a match.

"Stand back--close to the wall," he called as he dropped the burning mass on the red powder. In two or three leaps he joined us at the far end of the room.

Almost instantly a dazzling, intense flame broke out, and sizzled and crackled. With bated breath we watched.

It was almost incredible, but that glowing mass of powder seemed literally to be sinking, sinking right down into the cold steel. In tense silence we waited. On the ceiling we could still see the reflection of the molten mass in the cup which it had burned for itself in the top of the safe.

At last it fell through into the safe--fell as the burning roof of a frame building would fall into the building. No one spoke a word, but as we cautiously peered over the top of the safe we instinctively turned to Kennedy for an explanation. The Central Office man, with eyes as big as half-dollars, acted almost as if he would have liked to clap the irons on Kennedy. For there in the top of the safe was another hole, smaller but identical in nature with the first one.

"Thermit," was all Kennedy said.

"Thermit?" echoed Andrews, shifting the cigar which he had allowed to go out in the excitement.

"Yes, an invention of a chemist named Goldschmidt, of Essen, Germany. It is a compound of iron oxide, such as comes off a blacksmith's anvil or the rolls of a rolling-mill, and powdered metallic aluminum. You could thrust a red-hot bar into it without setting it off, but when you light a little magnesium powder and drop it on thermit, a combustion is started that quickly reaches fifty-four hundred degrees Fahrenheit. It has the peculiar property of concentrating its heat to the immediate spot on which it is placed. It is one of the most powerful oxidising agents known, and it doesn't even melt the rest of the steel surface. You see how it ate its way through the steel. Either black or red thermit will do the trick equally well."

No one said anything. There was nothing to say.

"Someone uncommonly clever, or instructed by someone uncommonly clever, must have done that job," added Craig. "Well, there is nothing more to be done here," he added, after a cursory look about the office. "Mr. Andrews, may I have a word with you? Come on, Jameson. Good day, Mr. Kahan. Good day, Officer."

Outside we stopped for a moment at the door of Andrews's car.

"I shall want to see Mr. Morowitch's papers at home," said Craig, "and also to call on Doctor Thornton. Do you think I shall have any difficulty?"

"Not at all," replied Mr. Andrews, "not at all. I will go with you myself and see that you have none. Say, Professor Kennedy," he broke out, "that was marvellous. I never dreamed such a thing was possible. But don't you think you could have learned something more up there in the office by looking around?"

"I did learn it," answered Kennedy. "The lock on the door was intact--whoever did the job let himself in by a key. There is no other way to get in."

Andrews gave a low whistle and glanced involuntarily up at the window with the sign of Morowitch & Co. in gold letters several floors above.

"Don't look up. I think that was Kahan looking out at us," he said, fixing his eyes on his cigar. "I wonder if he knows more about this than he has told! He was the 'company,' you know, but his interest in the business was only very slight. By George--"

"Not too fast, Mr. Andrews," interrupted Craig. "We have still to see Mrs. Morowitch and the doctor before we form any theories."

"A very handsome woman, too," said Andrews, as we seated ourselves in the car: "A good deal younger than Morowitch. Say, Kahan isn't a bad-looking chap, either, is he? I hear he was a very frequent visitor at his partner's house. Well, which first, Mrs. M. or the doctor?"

"The house," answered Craig.

Mr. Andrews introduced us to Mrs. Morowitch, who was in very deep mourning, which served, as I could not help noticing, rather to heighten than lessen her beauty. By contrast it brought out the rich deep colour of her face and the graceful lines of her figure. She was altogether a very attractive young widow.

She seemed to have a sort of fear of Andrews, whether merely because he represented the insurance company on which so much depended or because there were other

11

reasons for fear, I could not, of course, make out. Andrews was very courteous and polite, yet I caught myself asking if it was not a professional rather than a personal politeness. Remembering his stress on the fact that she was alone with her husband when he died, it suddenly flashed across my mind that somewhere I had read of a detective who, as his net was being woven about a victim, always grew more and more ominously polite toward the victim. I know that Andrews suspected her of a close connection with the case. As for myself, I don't know what I suspected as yet.

No objection was offered to our request to examine Mr. Morowitch's personal effects in the library, and accordingly Craig ransacked the desk and the letter-file. There was practically nothing to be discovered.

"Had Mr. Morowitch ever received any threats of robbery?" asked Craig, as he stood before the desk.

"Not that I know of," replied Mrs. Morowitch. "Of course every jeweller who carries a large stock of diamonds must be careful. But I don't think my husband had any special reason to fear robbery. At least he never said anything about it. Why do you ask?"

"Oh, nothing. I merely thought there might be some hint as to the motives of the robbery," said Craig. He was fingering one of those desk-calendars which have separate leaves for each day with blank spaces for appointments.

"'Close deal Poissan,'" he read slowly from one of the entries, as if to himself. "That's strange. It was the correspondence under the letter 'P' that was destroyed at the office, and there is nothing in the letter-file here, either. Who was Poissan?"

Mrs. Morowitch hesitated, either from ignorance or from a desire to evade the question. "A chemist, I think," she said doubtfully. "My husband had some dealings with him--some discovery he was going to buy. I don't know anything about it. I thought the deal was off."

"The deal?"

"Really, Mr. Kennedy, you had better ask Mr. Kahan. My husband talked very, little to me about business affairs."

"But what was the discovery?"

"I don't know. I only heard Mr. Morowitch and Mr. Kahan refer to some deal about a discovery regarding diamonds."

"Then Mr. Kahan knows about it?"

"I presume so."

"Thank you, Mrs. Morowitch," said Kennedy, when it was evident that she either could not or would not add anything to what she had said. "Pardon us for causing all this trouble."

"No trouble at all," she replied graciously, though I could see she was intent on every word and motion of Kennedy and Andrews.

Kennedy stopped the car at a drug-store a few blocks away and asked for the business telephone directory. In an instant, under chemists, he put his finger on the name of Poissan--"Henri Poissan, electric furnaces,--William St.," he read.

"I shall visit him to-morrow morning. Now for the doctor."

Doctor Thornton was an excellent specimen of the genus physician to the wealthy--polished, cool, suave. One of Mr. Andrews's men, as I have said, had seen him already, but the interview had been very unsatisfactory. Evidently, however, the doctor had been turning something over in his mind since then and had thought better of it. At any rate, his manner was cordial enough now.

As he closed the doors to his office, he began to pace the floor. "Mr. Andrews," he said, "I am in some doubt whether I had better tell you or the coroner what I know. There are certain professional secrets that a doctor must, as a duty to his patients, conceal. That is professional ethics. But there are also cases when, as a matter of public policy, a doctor should speak out."

He stopped and faced us.

"I don't mind telling you that I dislike the publicity that would attend any statement I might make to the coroner."

"Exactly," said Andrews. "I appreciate your position exactly. Your other patients would not care to see you involved in a scandal--or at least you would not care to have them see you so involved, with all the newspaper notoriety such a thing brings."

Doctor Thornton shot a quick glance at Andrews, as if he would like to know just how much his visitor knew or suspected.

Andrews drew a paper from his pocket. "This is a copy of the death-certificate," he said. "The Board of Health has furnished it to us. Our physicians at the insurance company tell me it is rather extraordinarily vague. A word from us calling the attention of the proper authorities to it would be sufficient, I think. But, Doctor, that is just the point. We do not desire publicity any more than you do. We could have the body of Mr. Morowitch exhumed and examined, but I prefer to get the facts in the case without resorting to such extreme measures."

"It would do no good," interrupted the doctor hastily. "And if you'll save me the publicity, I'll tell you why."

Andrews nodded, but still held the death-certificate where the doctor was constantly reminded of it.

"In that certificate I have put down the cause of death as congestion of the lungs due to an acute attack of pneumonia. That is substantially correct, as far as it goes. When I was summoned to see Mr. Morowitch I found him in a semiconscious state and scarcely breathing. Mrs. Morowitch told me that he had been brought home in a taxicab by a man who had picked him up on William Street. I'm frank to say that at first sight I thought it was a case of plain intoxication, for Mr. Morowitch sometimes indulged a little freely when he made a splendid deal. I smelled his breath, which was very feeble. It had a sickish sweet odour, but that did not impress me at the time. I applied my stethoscope to his lungs. There was a very marked congestion, and I made as my working diagnosis pneumonia. It was a case for quick and heroic action. In a very few minutes I had a tank of oxygen from the hospital.

"In the meantime I had thought over that sweetish odour, and it flashed on my mind that it might, after all, be a case of poisoning. When the oxygen arrived I administered it at once. As it happens, the Rockefeller Institute has just published a report of experiments with a new antidote for various poisons, which consists simply in a new method of enforced breathing and throwing off the poison by oxidising it in that way. In either case--the pneumonia theory or the poison theory--this line of action was the best that I could have adopted on the spur of the moment. I gave him some strychnine to strengthen his heart and by hard work I had him resting apparently a little easier. A nurse had been sent for, but had not arrived when a messenger came to me telling of a very sudden illness of Mrs. Morey, the wife of the steel-magnate. As the Morey home is only a half-block away, I left

Mr. Morowitch, with very particular instructions to his wife as to what to do.

"I had intended to return immediately, but before I got back Mr. Morowitch was dead. Now I think I've told you all. You see, it was nothing but a suspicion--hardly enough to warrant making a fuss about. I made out the death-certificate, as you see. Probably that would have been all there was to it if I hadn't heard of this incomprehensible robbery. That set me thinking again. There, I'm glad I've got it out of my system. I've thought about it a good deal since your man was here to see me."

"What do you suspect was the cause of that sweetish odour?" asked Kennedy.

The doctor hesitated. "Mind, it is only a suspicion. Cyanide of potassium or cyanogen gas; either would give such an odour."

"Your treatment would have been just the same had you been certain?"

"Practically the same, the Rockefeller treatment."

"Could it have been suicide" asked Andrews.

"There was no motive for it, I believe," replied the doctor.

"But was there any such poison in the Morowitch house?"

"I know that they were much interested in photography. Cyanide of potassium is used in certain processes in photography."

"Who was interested in photography, Mr. or Mrs. Morowitch?"

"Both of them."

"Was Mrs. Morowitch?"

"Both of them," repeated the doctor hastily. It was evident how Andrews's questions were tending, and it was also evident that the doctor did not wish to commit himself or even to be misunderstood.

Kennedy had sat silently for some minutes, turning the thing over in his mind. Apparently disregarding Andrews entirely, he now asked, "Doctor, supposing it had been cyanogen gas which caused the congestion of the lungs, and supposing it had not been inhaled in quantities large enough to kill outright, do you nevertheless feel that Mr. Morowitch was in a weak enough condition to die as a result of the congestion produced by the gas after the traces of the cyanogen had been perhaps thrown off?"

"That is precisely the impression which I wished to convey."

"Might I ask whether in his semiconscious state he said anything that might at all serve as a clue?"

"He talked ramblingly, incoherently. As near as I can remember it, he seemed to believe himself to have become a millionaire, a billionaire. He talked of diamonds, diamonds, diamonds. He seemed to be picking them up, running his fingers through them, and once I remember he seemed to want to send for Mr. Kahan and tell him something. 'I can make them, Kahan,' he said, 'the finest, the largest, the whitest--I can make them.'"

Kennedy was all attention as Dr. Thornton added this new evidence.

"You know," concluded the doctor, "that in cyanogen poisoning there might be hallucinations of the wildest kind. But then, too, in the delirium of pneumonia it might be the same."

I could see by the way Kennedy acted that for the first time a ray of light had dawned upon him in tracing out the case. As we rose to go, the doctor shook hands with us. His last words were said with an air of great relief, "Gentlemen, I have eased my conscience considerably."

As we parted for the night Kennedy faced Andrews. "You recall that you promised me one thing when I took up this case?" he asked.

Andrews nodded.

"Then take no steps until I tell you. Shadow Mrs. Morowitch and Mr. Kahan, but do not let them know you suspect them of anything. Let me run down this Poissan clue. In other words, leave the case entirely in my hands in other respects. Let me know any new facts you may unearth, and some time to-morrow I shall call on you, and we will determine what the next step is to be. Good night. I want to thank you for putting me in the way of this case. I think we shall all be surprised at the outcome."

It was late the following afternoon before I saw Kennedy again. He was in his laboratory winding two strands of platinum wire carefully about a piece of porcelain and smearing on it some peculiar black glassy granular substance that came in a sort of pencil, like a stick of sealing-wax. I noticed that he was very particular to keep the two wires exactly the same distance from each other throughout the entire length of the piece of porcelain, but I said nothing to distract his attention, though a thousand questions about the progress of the case were at my tongue's end.

Instead I watched him intently. The black substance formed a sort of bridge connecting and covering the wires. When he had finished he said: "Now you can ask me your questions, while I heat and anneal this little contrivance. I see you are bursting with curiosity."

"Well, did you see Poissan?" I asked.

Kennedy continued to heat the wire-covered porcelain. "I did, and he is going to give me a demonstration of his discovery to-night."

"His discovery!"

"You remember Morowitch's 'hallucination,' as the doctor called it? That was no hallucination; that was a

20

reality. This man Poissan says he has discovered a way to make diamonds artificially out of pure carbon in an electric furnace. Morowitch, I believe, was to buy his secret. His dream of millions was a reality--at least to him."

"And did Kahan and Mrs. Morowitch know it?" I asked quickly.

"I don't know yet," replied Craig, finishing the annealing.

The black glassy substance was now a dull grey.

"What's that stuff you were putting on the wire?" I asked.

"Oh, just a by-product made in the manufacture of sulphuric acid," answered Kennedy airily, adding, as if to change the subject: "I want you to go with me to-night. I told Poissan I was a professor in the university and that I would bring one of our younger trustees, the son of the banker, T. Pierpont Spencer, who might put some capital into his scheme. Now, Jameson, while I'm finishing up my work here, run over to the apartment and get my automatic revolver. I may need it to-night. I have communicated with Andrews, and he will be ready. The demonstration will take place at half-past-eight at Poissan's laboratory. I tried to get him to give it here, but he absolutely refused."

Half an hour later I rejoined Craig at his laboratory, and we rode down to the Great Eastern Life Building.

Andrews was waiting for us in his solidly furnished office. Outside I noted a couple of husky men, who seemed to be waiting for orders from their chief.

From the manner in which the vice-president greeted us it was evident that he was keenly interested in what Kennedy was about to do. "So you think Morowitch's deal was a deal to purchase the secret of diamond-making?" he mused.

"I feel sure of it," replied Craig. "I felt sure of it the moment I looked up Poissan and found that he was a manufacturer of electric furnaces. Don't you remember the famous Lemoine case in London and Paris?"

"Yes, but Lemoine was a fakir of the first water;" said Andrews. "Do you think this man is, too?"

"That's what I'm going to find out to-night before I take another step," said Craig. "Of course there can be no doubt that by proper use the electric furnace will make small, almost microscopic diamonds. It is not unreasonable to suppose that some day someone will be able to make large diamonds synthetically by the same process."

"Maybe this man has done it," agreed Andrews. "Who knows? I'll wager that if he has and that if Morowitch had bought an interest in his process Kahan knew of it. He's a sharp one. And Mrs. Morowitch doesn't let grass grow under her feet, when it comes to seeing the main chance as to money. Now just supposing Mr. Morowitch had bought an interest in a secret like that and supposing Kahan was in love with Mrs. Morowitch and that they--"

"Let us suppose nothing, Mr. Andrews," interrupted Kennedy. "At least not yet. Let me see; it is now ten minutes after eight. Poissan's place is only a few blocks from here. I'd like to get there a few minutes early. Let's start."

As we left the office, Andrews signalled to the two men outside, and they quietly followed a few feet in the rear, but without seeming to be with us.

Poissan's laboratory was at the top of a sort of loft building a dozen stories or so high. It was a peculiar building, with several entrances besides a freight elevator at the rear and fire-escapes that led to adjoining lower roofs.

We stopped around the corner in the shadow, and Kennedy and Andrews talked earnestly. As near as I could make out Kennedy was insisting that it would be best for Andrews and his men not to enter the building at all, but wait down-stairs while he and I went up. At last the arrangement was agreed on.

"Here," said Kennedy, undoing a package he had carried, "is a little electric bell with a couple of fresh dry batteries attached to it, and wires that will reach at least four hundred feet. You and the men wait in the shadow here by this side entrance for five minutes after Jameson and I go up. Then you must engage the night watchman in some way. While he is away you will find two wires dangling down the elevator shaft. Attach them to these wires from the bell and the batteries--these two--you know how to do that. The wires will be hanging in the third shaft--only one elevator is running at night, the first. The moment you hear the bell begin to ring; jump into the elevator and come up to the twelfth floor--we'll need you."

As Kennedy and I rode up in the elevator I could not help thinking what an ideal place a down-town office building is for committing a crime, even at this early hour of the evening. If the streets were deserted, the office-buildings were positively uncanny in their grim, black silence with only here and there a light.

The elevator in the first shaft shot down again to the ground floor, and as it disappeared Kennedy took two spools of wire from his pocket and hastily shoved them through the lattice work the third elevator shaft. They quickly unrolled, and I could hear them strike the top of the empty car below in the basement. That meant that Andrews on the ground floor could reach the wires and attach them to the bell.

Quickly in the darkness Kennedy attached the ends of the wires to the curious little coil I had seen him working on in the laboratory, and we proceeded down the hall to the rooms occupied by Poissan, Kennedy had allowed for the wire to reach from the elevator-shaft up this hall, also, and as he walked he paid it out in such a manner that it fell on the floor close to the wall, where, in the darkness, it would never be noticed or stumbled over.

Around an "L" in the hall I could see a ground-glass window with a light shining through it. Kennedy stopped at the window and quickly placed the little coil on the ledge, close up against the glass, with the wires running from it down the hall. Then we entered.

"On time to the minute, Professor," exclaimed Poissan, snapping his watch. "And this, I presume, is the banker who is interested in my great discovery of making artificial diamonds of any size or colour?" he added, indicating me.

"Yes," answered Craig, "as I told you, a son of Mr. T. Pierpont Spencer."

I shook hands with as much dignity as I could assume, for the role of impersonation was a new one to me.

Kennedy carelessly laid his coat and hat on the inside ledge of the ground-glass window, just opposite the spot where he had placed the little coil on the other side of the glass. I noted that the window was simply a large pane of wire-glass set in the wall for the purpose of admitting light in the daytime from the hall outside.

The whole thing seemed eerie to me--especially as Poissan's assistant was a huge fellow and had an evil look such as I had seen in pictures of the inhabitants of quarters of Paris which one does not frequent except in the company of a safe guide. I was glad Kennedy had brought his revolver, and rather vexed that he had not told me to do likewise. However, I trusted that Craig knew what he was about.

We seated ourselves some distance from a table on which was a huge, plain, oblong contrivance that reminded me of the diagram of a parallelopiped which had caused so much trouble in my solid geometry at college.

"That's the electric furnace, sir," said Craig to me with an assumed deference, becoming a college professor explaining things to the son of a great financier. "You see the electrodes at either end? When the current is turned on and led through them into the furnace you can get the most amazing temperatures in the crucible. The most refractory of chemical compounds can be broken up by that heat. What is the highest temperature you have attained, Professor?"

"Something over three thousand degrees Centigrade," replied Poissan, as he and his assistant busied themselves about the furnace.

We sat watching him in silence.

"Ah, gentlemen, now I am ready," he exclaimed at length, when everything was arranged to his satisfaction. "You see, here is a lump of sugar carbon--pure amorphous carbon: Diamonds, as you know, are composed of pure carbon crystallised under enormous pressure. Now, my theory is that if we can combine an enormous pressure and an enormous heat we can make diamonds artificially. The problem of pressure is the thing, for here in the furnace we

26

have the necessary heat. It occurred to me that when molten cast iron cools it exerts a tremendous pressure. That pressure is what I use."

"You know, Spencer, solid iron floats on molten iron like solid water--ice--floats on liquid water," explained Craig to me.

Poissan nodded. "I take this sugar carbon and place it in this soft iron cup. Then I screw on this cap over the cup, so. Now I place this mass of iron scraps in the crucible of the furnace and start the furnace."

He turned a switch, and long yellowish-blue sheets of flame spurted out from the electrodes on either side. It was weird, gruesome. One could feel the heat of the tremendous electric discharge.

As I looked at the bluish-yellow flames they gradually changed to a beautiful purple, and a sickish sweet odour filled the room. The furnace roared at first, but as the vapors increased it became a better conductor of the electricity, and the roaring ceased.

In almost no time the mass of iron scraps became molten. Suddenly Poissan plunged the cast-iron cup into the seething mass. The cup floated and quickly began to melt. As it did so he waited attentively until the proper moment. Then with a deft motion he seized the whole thing with a long pair of tongs and plunged it into a vat of running water. A huge cloud of steam filled the room.

I felt a drowsy sensation stealing over me as the sickish sweet smell from the furnace increased. Gripping the chair, I roused myself and watched Poissan attentively. He was working rapidly. As the molten mass cooled and solidified he took it out of the water and laid it on an anvil.

Then his assistant began to hammer it with careful, sharp blows, chipping off the outside.

"You see, we have to get down to the core of carbon gently," he said, as he picked up the little pieces of iron and threw them into a scrap-box. "First rather brittle cast iron, then hard iron, then iron and carbon, then some black diamonds, and in the very centre the diamonds.

"Ah! we are getting to them. Here is a small diamond. See, Mr. Spencer--gently Francois--we shall come to the large ones presently."

"One moment, Professor Poissan," interrupted Craig; "let your assistant break them out while I stand over him."

"Impossible. You would not know when you saw them. They are just rough stones."

"Oh, yes, I would."

"No, stay where you are. Unless I attend to it the diamonds might be ruined."

There was something peculiar about his insistence, but after he picked out the next diamond I was hardly prepared for Kennedy's next remark.

"Let me see the palms of your hands."

Poissan shot an angry glance at Kennedy, but he did not open his hands.

"I merely wish to convince you, 'Mr. Spencer,'" said Kennedy to me, "that it is no sleight-of-hand trick and that the professor has not several uncut stones palmed in his hand like a prestidigitator."

The Frenchman faced us, his face livid with rage. "You call me a prestidigitator, a fraud--you shall suffer for that! Sacrebleu! Ventre du Saint Gris! No man ever insults the honour of Poissan. Francois, water on the electrodes!"

The assistant dashed a few drops of water on the electrodes. The sickish odour increased tremendously. I felt myself almost going, but with an effort I again roused myself. I wondered how Craig stood the fumes, for I suffered an intense headache and nausea.

"Stop!" Craig thundered. "There's enough cyanogen in this room already. I know your game--the water forms acetylene with the carbon, and that uniting with the nitrogen of the air under the terrific heat of the electric arc forms hydrocyanic acid. Would you poison us, too? Do you think you can put me unconscious out on the street and have a society doctor diagnose my case as pneumonia? Or do you think we shall die quietly in some hospital as a certain New York banker did last year after he had watched an alchemist make silver out of apparently nothing!"

The effect on Poissan was terrible. He advanced toward Kennedy, the veins in his face fairly standing out. Shaking his forefinger, he shouted: "You know that, do you? You are no professor, and this is no banker. You are spies, spies. You come from the friends of Morowitch, do you? You have gone too far with me."

Kennedy said nothing, but retreated and took his coat and hat off the window ledge. The hideous penetrating light of the tongues of flame from the furnace played on the ground-glass window.

Poissan laughed a hollow laugh.

"Put down your hat and coat, Mistair Kennedy," he hissed. "The door has been locked ever since you have been here. Those windows are barred, the telephone wire is cut, and it is three hundred feet to the street. We shall leave you here when the fumes have overcome you. Francois and I can stand them up to a point, and when we reach that point we are going."

Instead of being cowed Kennedy grew bolder, though I, for my part, felt so weakened that I feared the outcome of a hand-to-hand encounter with either Poissan or Francois, who appeared as fresh as if nothing had happened. They were hurriedly preparing to leave us.

"That would do you no good," Kennedy rejoined, "for we have no safe full of jewels for you to rob. There are no keys to offices to be stolen from our pockets. And let me tell you--you are not the only man in New York who knows the secret of thermite. I have told the secret to the police, and they are only waiting to find who destroyed Morowitch's correspondence under the letter 'P' to apprehend the robber of his safe. Your secret is out."

"Revenge! revenge!" Poissan cried. "I will have revenge. Francois, bring out the jewels--ha! ha!--here in this bag are the jewels of Mr. Morowitch. To-night Francois and I will go down by the back elevator to a secret exit. In two hours all your police in New York cannot find us. But in two hours you two impostors will be suffocated--perhaps you will die of cyanogen, like Morowitch, whose jewels I have at last."

He went to the door into the hall and stood there with a mocking laugh. I moved to make a rush toward them, but Kennedy raised his hand.

"You will suffocate," Poissan hissed again.

Just then we heard the elevator door clang, and hurried steps came down the long hall.

Craig whipped out his automatic and began pumping the bullets out in rapid succession. As the smoke cleared I expected to see Poissan and Francois lying on the floor. Instead, Craig had fired at the lock of the door. He had shattered it into a thousand bits. Andrews and his men were running down the hall.

"Curse you!" muttered Poissan as he banged the now useless lock, "who let those fellows in? Are you a wizard?"

Craig smiled coolly as the ventilation cleared the room of the deadly cyanogen.

"On the window-sill outside is a selenium cell. Selenium is a bad conductor of electricity in the dark, and an excellent conductor when exposed to light. I merely moved my coat and hat, and the light from the furnace which was going to suffocate us played through the glass on the cell, the circuit was completed without your suspecting that I could communicate with friends outside, a bell was rung on the street, and here they are. Andrews, there is the murderer of Morowitch, and there in his hands are the Morowitch--"

Poissan had moved toward the furnace. With a quick motion he seized the long tongs. There was a cloud of choking vapour. Kennedy leaped to the switch and shut off the current. With the tongs he lifted out a shapeless piece of valueless black graphite.

"All that is left of the priceless Morowitch jewels," he exclaimed ruefully. "But we have the murderer."

"And to-morrow a certified check for one hundred thousand dollars goes to Mrs. Morowitch with my humblest apologies and sympathy," added Andrews. "Professor Kennedy, you have earned your retainer."